Open Centipede!

By Michael Anthony Steele

Scholastic Inc.

New York   Toronto   London   Auckland   Sydney

Mexico City   New Delhi   Hong Kong   Buenos Aires

ISBN: 0-439-59718-8

Published by Scholastic Inc.
SCHOLASTIC and associated logos are trademarks and/or registered trademarks of Scholastic Inc.

12 11 10 9 8 7 6 5 4 3 2 1   4 5 6 7 8/0

Designed by John Daly
Printed in the U.S.A.
First printing, December 2004

ONE

Shrek stared at the man sitting in his living room. He didn't understand why such a scary ogre as himself should be so uncomfortable around a mere human in the first place. After all, *he* wasn't out of place — he was in his own home. Yet Shrek didn't know what to do.

"So . . . uh . . ." Shrek tugged at his shirt collar. "How about this weather?"

Prince Phillip looked up from his untouched drink. "It's unseasonably warm," he replied. "Don't you think?"

Shrek took a sip from his own drink. Then he casually twirled the eyeball garnish with two of his stubby green fingers. "Yes, it's very . . . warm." After another unpleasant pause, Shrek nodded toward the dinner table. "Do you think we should wake her up?"

Prince Phillip followed his gaze until both stared at the dinner table. Sleeping Beauty snored loudly as her head lay on her plate of untouched food. Her left nostril blew tiny bubbles in the sauce with every exhale. Fiona quietly removed some of the dirty dishes, trying not to wake the snoozing princess.

Prince Phillip rolled his eyes. "I suppose I should revive her before she sucks another bean up her nose."

As the prince went over to wake his slumbering bride, Shrek sighed and stared at his drink some more. It had been the same awkwardness all through dinner. Even when Sleeping Beauty *wasn't* passed out on her pork chops, no one hardly said a word to one another. Shrek and Fiona had nothing in common with the royal couple. It was all extremely uncomfortable. In fact, it reminded Shrek of the last time he sat through an awkward dinner with a royal pair — Fiona's parents. However, Shrek and Fiona's father had gotten into a fight. It wasn't fun, but it was certainly livelier than this event.

"Wake up, dear," the prince said as he gently nudged Sleeping Beauty. She continued snoring. "Darling?" He gave her shoulder a shake. "Pumpkin?" He shook her harder. Then he took a deep breath and yelled, "WAKE UP!"

Shrek and Fiona jumped with a start. The princess slowly sat up and yawned. The left side of her face was covered in sauce and beans. "Oh, did I doze off again?" she asked. A few beans fell from her face and plopped onto her plate.

"I'm afraid so, honeybunch," the prince replied through clenched teeth. As he helped her stand, he sighed and looked at Shrek. "We'd better be going."

Shrek sprang to his feet and bounded toward the hat rack. He snatched the couple's cloaks and hats. "Aw, really? So soon?"

"I'm afraid so," Prince Phillip replied. He helped the drowsy Sleeping Beauty stumble away from the table. With his free hand, he took the garments from Shrek.

When the ogre opened the door for them, the prince poked his head outside. "Come on, kids!" he called. "It's time to go!"

Shrek heard the galloping of hoofed feet. Donkey leaped through the doorway of Shrek's tree-stump cabin.

"There," said Donkey, "that's the last ride you're going to get!"

Shrek bent over. "Who are you talking to?" he asked.

Donkey turned his head and stared at his back. "They fell off again?"

Both Shrek and Donkey gazed though the front door to see a young boy and girl lying in a heap in front of the cabin. Their eyes were closed and both snored very loudly.

"That's quite all right," said the prince. "I'll get them on the way out." He laughed nervously. "They take after their mother, I'm afraid."

"Thanks for coming," Fiona whispered, trying not to wake the princess, who seemed asleep once more. "We'll have to do it again sometime."

Sleeping Beauty popped her head up. "Thank you so much for inviting us," she slurred. Then she poked Shrek in the chest with a finger. "And I'm not mad anymore about that *Sleeping Ugly* story you made up. It's actually quite funny when you think about . . ." Her head tipped back and a loud snore growled from her open mouth. She was out again.

Prince Phillip shrugged and placed both hats on his head. He hung the cloaks over one arm and threw Sleeping Beauty over his shoulder. Her snoring didn't skip a beat. He extended his free hand toward Shrek. "Yes, uh . . . we *will* have to do it again sometime."

"Sure," said Shrek. He examined the prince's cumbersome load. "Do you need any help?"

"No, I'm used to it," Prince Phillip replied as he walked over to the kids. He reached down and heaved them off the ground by the back of their clothing. Their little arms and legs dangled as they continued to snore loudly. Prince Phillip slowly lugged his sleeping family out of the swamp.

"Bye-bye," Donkey said through a forced grin.

"See you later," Shrek said through a forced smile of his own.

Shrek smiled and waved until the prince and his snoozing family were far down the trail out of his swamp. Then he slammed the door and returned to his chair. He picked up his drink and downed it in one gulp. "Promise me we'll *never* do that again," he told Fiona.

Donkey collapsed by the fire. "Tell me about it," he added. "My back is killing me. Do you have some aspirin or something?"

Fiona looked shocked. "What are you talking about?" she asked. "I had a great time! Granted, I wasn't expecting her to pass out every few minutes when I invited them."

"Hello?" asked Shrek. "Her name is *Sleeping* Beauty!" He threw his hands up. "It was a complete disaster."

"I'm with Shrek on this one," Donkey agreed. "I didn't mind sitting at the kiddie table during dinner. But if I'd known there were going to be donkey rides at this little get-together, I wouldn't have come."

"Well, didn't you and Prince Phillip talk about anything?" Fiona asked Shrek.

"Let's see . . . when we weren't making small talk and discussing the weather, for the twentieth time," Shrek snapped, "all he did was ask me about different remedies for snoring."

"Well, *I* had a good time." Fiona crossed her arms. "I think we should have guests more often."

Shrek got to his feet. "Ogres don't like guests. We like to be alone. Ogres are solitary creatures. That's it. End of story."

Fiona stepped closer to Shrek and took his hands. "I enjoy being alone with you, too. But it's fun to have guests over once in a while."

"I'm a guest!" Donkey grinned. "Don't I count?"

"She said 'once in a while,' Donkey." Shrek patted him on the head. "You're over here so much we're thinking of painting you to match the furniture."

"Come on," Fiona continued. "Maybe our next dinner guests will be more lively."

Shrek sighed. "All right. Who else did you have in mind?"

Fiona thought for a moment. "How about the Three Pigs?"

"They'll want to remodel the place," Shrek replied. "Next."

"Hansel and Gretel?"

"We'll be sweeping up bread crumbs for weeks," said Shrek.

Fiona thought harder. "We could always invite someone from the village."

"And just who would that be?" Shrek asked. "The ones who want to burn us, or the ones who want to stick us with pitchforks?"

"I'm sure there's a nice family in the village who wants to be friends," Fiona replied. "Besides, once they get to know us, maybe they won't chase us anymore."

"That won't matter," Shrek replied. "Villagers are all

the same. You stay out of their way, they come looking for you. You scare them away, and even *more* come looking for you. And if you're nice to them and help them, they'll stay away for a while, but sooner or later —"

"Help them?" Fiona asked. "The villagers?"

Donkey's ears perked up. "Don't tell me you helped them once, Shrek? You?"

Shrek's ear stalks drooped and he looked embarrassed. "That was a long time ago."

"You never told me about that," said Fiona. "What happened?"

Donkey scrambled to his feet and trotted over to Shrek. "Ooh, tell us a story!"

"Yes," Fiona agreed. "Tell us what you did."

Shrek let out a huge sigh and plopped down in his favorite chair. "All right. Long, long ago —"

"Hey, wait a minute," Donkey interrupted. "Who ever heard of a story starting with 'long, long ago'? You're supposed to say 'once upon a time.'"

"Okay, okay!" yelled Shrek. "Once upon a time . . ."

TWO

"When I was much younger," Shrek began, "I lived all alone in my swamp. I had everything I needed: plenty of food, shelter, and solitude. The tastiest slugs, swamp toads, and weed rats were only a short walk away. But there was one dish that was hard to come by — green-ring toadstools."

Donkey grimaced. "That sounds more like a disease than food."

"Oh, they're quite delicious," said Shrek. "The trouble is, they only grow in early spring and on the outskirts of the swamp. . . ."

One spring afternoon, Shrek decided to gather some delicious green-ring toadstools. He stomped to the edge of the swamp in search of the tasty treat. However, as he neared the outer rim of his property, he found himself very close to the neighboring village. Knowing how villagers and ogres don't mix, he had always tried to avoid them whenever possible. But since green-ring toadstools were so rare, he decided to take a chance. Shrek quietly continued his search, trying not to alert any of the villagers.

As he went on, he came across a wooden sign nailed to a tree. Apparently, the villagers were having trouble with a local thief. BIG REWARD! the sign read. CAPTURE THE BANDIT! DEAD OR ALIVE!

Shrek kept walking and didn't give much thought to the sign. After all, it was the villagers' problem, not his. His only concern right then was hunting for green-ring toadstools. But he wasn't having much luck.

He was just about to give up his search and go home when he smelled something absolutely scrumptious.

The ogre followed the scent to the back of a small cottage at the edge of the village. The rear window was open and a warm blueberry pie sat on the windowsill. Shrek inhaled the wonderful aroma and dared to step closer to the cabin. It wasn't the smell of the pie that enticed him, though. Beneath the window, Shrek spotted a small cluster of toadstools. A bright green ring circled each of their long stalks. Their pungent odor made the ogre's mouth water.

Shrek tiptoed closer to the cottage. He didn't think anyone would mind if he picked the toadstools. They were poisonous to everyone but ogres, anyway. To him, their toxin gave their flavor a delectable kick stronger than one hundred chili peppers.

Shrek placed one hand on the windowsill while he bent over and began plucking them from the ground. Just then, he felt tiny feet race over his hand. He quickly stood and saw a little squirrel standing on his arm, staring back at him. It was the strangest squirrel he'd ever seen. The rodent wore a black mask around his eyes. He also carried a small brown sack and had a tiny sword tucked into a red sash around his waist.

"Just what kind of squirrel are you?" Shrek asked the tiny animal.

The squirrel dropped his sack and drew his sword. "I am the worst kind!" he replied in a shrill voice. His bushy tail flicked twice. "I'm armed and dangerous!"

Shrek shoved the toadstools into his pocket and brought his arm closer to his face. The squirrel balanced on the ogre's sleeve like a parrot.

"Well, you're certainly armed," Shrek said with a chuckle. "And you might be dangerous to a field mouse or a small bird."

The squirrel dropped his sword and began to tremble with fear.

"Now, don't be scared, little fella," said Shrek. "I only wanted to get a closer look at you."

The squirrel turned and sprang off Shrek's arm. Instead of hitting the ground, he landed on the edge of the pie pan. The blueberry pie catapulted toward Shrek and hit him square in the face. *SPLAT!*

The tiny rodent fell to the yard below and ran away. Shrek scraped pieces of pie away from his mouth and eyes. The rest of his face was covered with dark blue filling. It wrapped around his bald head like a mask.

After spitting out the last of the crust, Shrek bent down and snatched up the sword and small sack the squirrel was carrying. "You forgot your bag and your wee sword," Shrek called out, but the furry-tailed rodent had disappeared into the swamp.

Wondering what a masked squirrel would be hauling, Shrek reached into the sack and pulled out a brass goblet. *What would he need with a cup like this?* Shrek wondered.

A bloodcurdling scream erupted behind him. Shrek spun around to see a man and woman staring out the window. Their faces were frozen in horror.

The man pointed toward the cup in Shrek's hand. "It's the bandit!" he yelled.

Taken by surprise, Shrek dropped the sword and brass goblet. "Now wait a minute!"

The woman continued to scream as the man ran out of the front of the cabin and into the street. "Help! It's the bandit! It's the bandit!"

"I'll tell you what," Shrek said as he backed away. "I'll just be on my way. No harm, no foul."

Shrek could still hear the villagers' screams as he dashed into the swamp.

THREE

When Shrek felt he was far enough away from the village, he stopped and ripped leaves from a nearby fern. He balled them up and used them as a towel, wiping the remaining bits of pie from his face.

He heard voices nearby. "That was quick," he whispered to himself. "Usually it takes the villagers half the day to round up an angry mob."

Shrek knelt and parted the branches of two large bushes. He was surprised to see that the voices weren't coming from a mob of villagers. Instead, he saw the little squirrel he'd frightened, along with a much larger squirrel by a rocky outcropping at the base of a small hill. The bigger one wore an eye patch over one eye and a sword tucked under a sash around his waist.

"You just ran away?" the larger squirrel asked. "From one measly ogre?"

"There was nothing I could do, Captain," the first squirrel pleaded. "The beast snapped my sword in half and threatened to chew me into goo!"

"Why, that lying little . . ." Shrek said to himself as he began to stand. However, he quickly knelt again when he heard a rustling nearby.

Three more squirrels emerged from the undergrowth. There were two thin ones and one chubby one. They each wore black masks, had swords tucked in sashes, and carried large bags over their shoulders.

The captain addressed the new arrivals. "My brother bandits," he said with a flick of his bushy tail. "It seems we have a coward among us. Not only did a mere ogre scare him out of his sword, but, more important, out of his plunder of the day!"

The other squirrels grumbled with dissatisfaction.

The captain of the squirrels placed a furry paw on the shoulder of the trembling bandit. "Maybe our brother has forgotten what we do with cowards," said the captain. "Care to remind him?"

"Run and squeal, spin the wheel!" the three squirrels chanted. "Run and squeal, spin the wheel!"

Shrek watched as the three squirrels moved some dried brush away from the rocky outcropping. To his surprise, they revealed a crudely made carnival wheel attached to a wooden stand. The wheel was sectioned off like a pie with each piece painted a different color. Small pegs lined the outside and a wooden arrow jutted down from the top of the stand, pointing to the colorful circle. Short phrases were written in each section, including WHOA-NELLY, UPSY-DOWNSY, PADDY WAGON, and CAPTAIN'S CHOICE.

"Please," the first squirrel begged. "Not the —"

"That's right!" the captain interrupted. "The Wheel of Misfortune!"

Still trembling, the offending squirrel stumbled to the wheel and gave it a timid spin. Each of the tiny pegs slapped against the arrow as it turned.

Click-click-click-click-click-click-click . . .

When the wheel slowly came to a stop, the arrow pointed to a section labeled UP, UP, AND AWAY.

The squirrel's eyes widened in horror. "Oh, please no! Not Up, Up, and Away!" he pleaded. "Anything but Up, Up, and Away!"

The captain drew his sword and pointed toward the frightened squirrel. "The wheel has spoken!"

The three others quickly scampered up a nearby sapling. When they reached the top, their weight caused the small tree to bend over until its tip touched the ground just behind the guilty squirrel. The captain stepped closer and jabbed his sword at the frightened squirrel, causing him to back up.

When the little squirrel stepped onto the tip of the

bent tree, the captain's one visible eye flashed with wicked delight. "Up . . . up . . ." he said, "and *away*!"

The three squirrels hopped off the bent tree and it snapped back upright. As the tip whipped upward, it catapulted the tiny squirrel and flung him high into the sky. The small bandit squealed as he sailed over the treetops and out of sight.

Shrek actually felt a bit sorry for the squirrel. After all, if it weren't for him scaring the little rodent, he wouldn't have been given the old Up, Up, and Away.

The captain returned his sword to his belt as the other squirrels picked up their sacks. Then he stepped up to one of the large boulders and did something unexpected. He said a special phrase and the boulder magically rolled aside, revealing a hidden cave!

"Go on," the captain barked. "Store your sacks and be done with it!" He glanced around suspiciously. "We still have much work to do."

Shrek watched in amazement as the four squirrels stepped inside and the boulder rolled back into place.

FOUR

"You have got to be kidding me," said Donkey. "This has to be the craziest story I've ever heard."

Fiona stood and began to clear the dinner table. "You have to admit, dear," she said, "it *is* a little hard to believe."

"It's all true," Shrek assured them, raising one green hand. "I saw it for myself."

Shrek stood and helped Fiona finish cleaning up by grabbing a couple of dirty plates and a half-eaten bowl of insect party mix. He set the plates in the sink but held onto the bowl. He reached in and grabbed a handful of beetle crisps and assorted bugs. He popped them into his mouth with a crunch.

"First of all," said Donkey, "who ever heard of a talking squirrel?"

"Who ever heard of a talking Donkey?" Shrek shot back.

Donkey thought for a moment. "Well, that's . . . that's different!" He clomped toward them and placed his front hooves on the table. "Okay, Mister Story-man, if it's all true, then what was the magic password?"

"Oh, that?" Shrek asked. He thought for a moment. "Let's see . . . it was *Open* . . ." Shrek reached into the bowl and pulled out a squirming centipede. His eyes lit up and he quickly slurped up the long insect. "Cen-tipede. That's it. *Open Centipede!*"

Donkey raised an eyebrow, looking dubious. "*Open Centipede*, eh? You making this up, Shrek?"

Shrek chewed on his centipede slowly. "Do you want to hear the rest of my story or not?"

Donkey's ears perked up. "I suppose if I can believe

in talking squirrels, *Open Centipede* is no biggie. So . . . what happened next?"

Shrek continued to crouch behind the bushes. He watched as the boulder rolled away once more and the four bandit squirrels strode out of the cave. Each of their sacks was now empty. As the boulder rolled shut behind them, the squirrels disappeared into the swamp.

When he could no longer hear their tiny footsteps, Shrek stood and slowly approached the hidden cave. Curiosity got the best of him and he had to try out the password for himself.

Shrek raised his hands as if he were a magician casting a spell. *"Open Centipede!"*

The boulder slowly rolled to the side, revealing the mouth of a hidden cave. Shrek bent down and cautiously stepped inside.

A shaft of light streamed through a small hole at

the top of the cave. It shone on the long stalactites that jutted down from the ceiling. Cobwebs stretched across them and tiny insects skittered over the walls. The inside looked like any other cave — except for one thing. From floor to ceiling, the cave was filled with all sorts of . . . junk!

"What in the world?" Shrek mumbled as he scanned the piles heaped around him. There were pots, pans, cups, clothes, toys, tools, and even a large blacksmith's anvil. "What would a bunch of squirrels want with this stuff?"

Then Shrek noticed something familiar. "Hey!" He reached into one of the piles and pulled out a large, beat-up frying pan. "I thought I'd lost this months ago." A few items from the pile fell to his feet. "Those bushy-tailed rats must have stolen it from me!"

As even more pieces of junk fell from the pile, Shrek realized he had started a small avalanche. He backed out of the cave with a few quick steps — just in time! The entire pile fell over and littered junk everywhere. Then the large boulder rolled back. It crushed a few dishes as it locked in place. Shrek looked at his recovered pan, smiled, and headed for home.

That night, Shrek sautéed the toadstools in his skillet. The smell of them simmering in slug oil made his mouth water. He couldn't wait to pour the finished sauce over his duck-feet loaf.

As the toadstools were cooking to the peak of perfection, a loud banging rattled Shrek's door. Irritated, Shrek pulled the pan off the fire and carried it with him as he stomped to the front of his cabin. The oil continued to crackle as he flung open the door.

To his annoyance, a small angry mob stood outside. The villagers held burning torches, sharpened pitchforks, and other menacing-looking farming tools. They growled and grumbled as they aimed their weapons at the ogre.

FIVE

Not at all frightened, Shrek casually stepped outside. This took the villagers by surprise and they backed away. He glanced down at his pan of toadstools. "Gee, if I knew you were coming, I would have made more."

His casual attitude seemed to make the villagers even more nervous. They took another step back and lowered their weapons slightly. One man — the man from the cabin — swallowed hard and pointed at Shrek. "That's him," he said. "That's the thief!"

"I'm not a thief," Shrek protested. The villagers

looked at one another and seemed to scrape together some courage. They raised their pitchforks again. Shrek held up one hand. "Hold on," he said. "Wait a minute now."

Another man pointed to Shrek's hand. "That's my Mildred's frying pan, that is!"

Shrek looked down at the skillet containing the cooling toadstools. "What are you talking about?" he asked. "This is mine!"

"No, it's not!" the man argued. "It's my wife's!"

Shrek cocked his head. "And what makes you say that?"

The man's eyes darted nervously. "Well, it's . . . it's round," he stammered. "It has a long handle and . . . and you can cook with it."

"You're right," said Shrek sarcastically. "No other frying pan would fit that description."

"Let's get him!" someone yelled. The villagers took a step forward.

"Now hang on a minute," said Shrek. "I'm not the thief, but I can tell you who is."

They glared at him skeptically. "Oh, yeah?" asked the man from the cabin. "Who is it, then?"

Shrek told them about his run-in with the squirrel behind the cabin. He also described what happened with the other squirrels he'd seen.

"You expect us to believe that?" the man asked.

"It's the truth," said Shrek.

Another man stepped forward. He wore a black leather apron and held a large steel mallet. "What about my missing anvil?" he asked. "Do you expect me to believe a squirrel carried it away?"

Shrek thought for moment. He wasn't sure how to explain that one. "Well, there were five of them."

The villagers took another step forward, until they were all gathered around Shrek in a tight semicircle. "You're the thief, ogre, and you know it," another one said.

Shrek had heard about enough of their accusations. "Well, I only have one thing to say to that!" He took a deep breath and let loose one of his loudest, most bloodcurdling roars.

ROOOOOOOOOOOOOOOOOOOOOAAAAA-AAAAAAARRRRRRRRRRRRRRRRRRRRRRRR!

The villagers choked and gagged after getting a face full of the ogre's rancid breath. Some of their hair was curled and singed while two of them passed out completely. The small group picked up their fallen comrades, then stumbled away from Shrek's cabin. He heard them hacking and coughing long after they were out of sight.

When they were gone, Shrek looked down at the sautéed toadstools. They sat lifelessly in the pan, cold and limp. His dinner was ruined.

The next morning, Shrek set out in search of more toadstools. Now that his last batch had been spoiled, his craving for them had only increased. He didn't care if he had to return to the outskirts of the village. He wouldn't let the villagers ruin another dinner. He would find some more toadstools if it was the last thing he did.

As he neared the edge of the swamp, he spotted another wanted sign. This one was quite different from the one he'd seen the day before. This sign had a rough drawing of him on it. Below the crude drawing were the words THIEVING OGRE. Above the drawing was the phrase WANTED: DEAD or ALIVE.

"That's just great," Shrek said to himself. Now he would never get a moment's peace. The villagers would organize lynch mobs every night. Each night more of them would come. Soon there would be so many that a mere stinky roar wouldn't be enough to frighten them away. He needed to do something about this situation before it got worse.

Shrek abandoned his search for the toadstools. Instead, he headed for the secret cave. He would gather as many of the stolen items as possible and return them to the village. He didn't care if they thought he was a thief or not. But maybe they would leave him alone if he brought their stuff back.

After trudging through the dense underbrush, Shrek spotted the small hill. He thought about crouching and sneaking up to the cave, just in case the bandits were there. But he quickly dismissed that idea. If the thieves were there, even better. Then he could grab a couple of the mischievous squirrels as well. That would show the villagers.

But as Shrek walked closer to the cave, he didn't see a single bandit squirrel. All was quiet and the large boulder covered the entrance as before.

"*Open Centipede,*" he said. The large rock magically rolled aside.

Shrek stepped into the cave and immediately found a large empty sack. He stuffed it full of as much loot as possible. *This should be enough for now,* he thought. *I'll tell them where the cave is and they can get the rest themselves.*

Shrek was about to exit the cave when he spied the large anvil. Remembering the blacksmith, the ogre picked up the heavy hunk of iron and shoved it under one arm. He threw the hefty bag over the other shoulder, then turned toward the entrance.

The boulder suddenly rolled back into place. Shrek dropped the sack and the anvil and pushed against the large stone, but it was too late. The boulder locked shut with a loud *CLUNK!*

That's all right, Shrek thought. *I'm sure the password works from the inside, too.* Shrek took a deep breath and said, "Open . . ."

Something was wrong.

"Open . . ."

He had forgotten the password.

"Open . . . !"

Shrek was trapped inside.

"You forgot the password?" Donkey asked. He clopped closer to Shrek and Fiona as they washed dishes. "You just *said* the password to get *inside* the cave."

"I was irritated," Shrek replied as he dried the last dish and handed it to Fiona. "It just slipped my mind, that's all."

"It was *centipede*," said Donkey. "*Cen. Ti. Pede!* You can't get any simpler than that."

"Weren't there any real centipedes crawling around the cave?" asked Fiona. "If you'd seen them, they would have reminded you."

"It was a musty old cave in the middle of a swamp," Shrek replied. "It was infested with all kinds of creepy-crawlies." He sank down in his chair with a sigh. "And believe me, I tried them all."

Inside the dark cave, Shrek sat on the large anvil. The sack of loot was on the ground beside him. He sighed and scratched the back of his head.

"*Open Swamp Spider!*" he said. The boulder didn't move. "*Open Stinkbug!*" Nothing happened. "*Open Slime Beetle!*" Still nothing.

A noise from outside the cave caught his attention — the sound of clinking metal and tiny footsteps. One of the squirrels had returned.

"*Open Centipede!*" said a shrill voice. The large boulder began to roll away from the entrance.

Shrek snapped his fingers. "I was just getting to centipede!" He jumped to his feet and grabbed the anvil. He threw it under one arm and flung the sack over his shoulder. When the doorway was completely open, Shrek stepped outside to find a very surprised squirrel.

"Halt, thief!" ordered the chubby squirrel. He dropped his small sack and drew his sword.

"You're one to call someone a thief," Shrek replied.

This little crook wasn't frightened like the first squirrel Shrek had met. He took a step closer. "You will relinquish our property immediately!"

Shrek set down the sack and the anvil and leaned over until he was face-to-face with the small bandit. "My, such big words for a wee little rodent."

This squirrel had no fear. He leaped forward and slashed his sword at the ogre's face. Shrek jerked back just in time to avoid getting a nasty cut across his nose.

"Hey, now," Shrek yelled. "That's not very nice!"

He reached down and flicked the squirrel with one plump green finger. The little thief tumbled into the cave just as the boulder rolled back into place.

"There," said Shrek. "That'll hold you."

He picked up his load and lumbered into the

swamp. Unfortunately, he was only a few feet away when the bottom of the sack ripped and its contents spilled onto the ground. Shrek grumbled as he knelt to pick up what he could.

While he was crouched behind some bushes, he heard more squirrels approaching. He parted the shrubs and saw the squirrel with the eye patch followed by the two thin ones. All of them hefted heavy sacks over their shoulders.

The leader stopped in front of the cave. *"Open Centipede!"* he said in his tiny — yet oddly commanding — voice. Once again, the large rock rolled aside.

As soon as the opening was clear, the chubby squirrel ran out. "Thief! Thief!" he cried.

"Yes," answered the captain, "we are all thieves here. What's your point?"

"No," said the squirrel. "Another thief! One that stole from *us!*"

"What?" screeched the captain. He dropped his sack and drew his sword. The other two did the same.

The chubby squirrel described how Shrek had made off with their loot.

"And you did nothing to stop this ogre?" the captain asked.

"No," snapped the squirrel. "I mean, yes, I did something. I attacked him immediately."

The captain looked around. "I don't see his lifeless body lying around."

"Well . . ." said the portly squirrel. "I missed and he got away."

"He *what?*" the captain bellowed.

"And he took a sack of loot from the cave," the squirrel added.

The captain bared his pointy little teeth. "Do you know what this means?"

The squirrel hung his head. "Let someone in, give the wheel a spin," he muttered.

"Let someone in, give the wheel a spin!" the two skinny squirrels chanted. "Let someone in, give the wheel a spin!" They scampered to the side of the cave and pulled the branches away from the wheel. The portly squirrel shuffled forward and gave it a spin.

Click-click-click-click-click-click-click . . . click . . . click . . . click.

The wheel came to a stop with the arrow pointing to a section labeled WHOA-NELLY.

The plump squirrel's eyes widened. "Not Whoa-Nelly!" he cried. "Anything but Whoa-Nelly!"

"Whoa-Nelly?" Shrek whispered to himself. He watched as the two thin squirrels flicked their tails and scampered into the swamp. He heard a violent rustling of branches and leaves followed by growling and hissing. The two squirrels backed into the clearing pulling two long ropes. They tugged harder until a snarling badger emerged from the bushes. It snapped at them with sharp teeth and struggled against the cords looped around its neck.

The captain of the bandits reached into his sack and pulled out another length of rope. He quickly tied the chunky squirrel's front paws together. He made a loop at the other end and lassoed it around the badger's neck. Then he grabbed the portly squirrel and tossed him onto the animal's back. The wild beast jumped and kicked like a bucking bronco. The other two squirrels released their ropes, and the badger bounded into the swamp.

"Whoa-Nelly!" yelled the squirrel as he rode the badger. "Whoa-Nelly! *Whoa-Nelly!*"

Soon both badger and squirrel were out of sight. The remaining miniature bandits picked up their bags and marched into the cave. When the boulder rolled back into place, Shrek grabbed the anvil and as many of the spilled items as he could hold. With his awkward load, he slowly made his way to the village.

SEVEN

"Now I *know* this story isn't true," said Donkey. "Who ever heard of a bucking-bronco badger?" Donkey swished his tail as he sat between the two ogres' chairs.

"It's all true, I swear," Shrek promised.

"Man, you really had me going," Donkey replied with a smirk. "With the squirrel bandits and their tiny swords and the secret cave."

Shrek frowned. "Well, if you don't believe me, there's no point in finishing the story, is there?"

"You have to finish the story," said Fiona.

"Why should I?" asked Shrek. He glared at Donkey. "After all, it's just a fairy tale, right?"

Donkey got to his feet. "I didn't say it was a fairy tale."

Shrek crossed his arms and turned his head. "It must be if the story isn't true." He gave Fiona a small wink.

Donkey's ears drooped. "But I want to know what happened to the squirrels and the villagers."

"Why?" asked Shrek. "It's just a story."

Donkey sighed. "Okay, I believe you."

Shrek cupped a hand behind one of his ear stalks. "What was that?"

"I said I believe you," growled Donkey. "Are you happy now?"

Shrek leaned back and smiled. "Quite happy."

"So tell us what happened next," said Fiona.

Shrek thought for a moment. "Well, let's just say that Donkey isn't the only one who had trouble believing this story."

By late afternoon, Shrek reached the village with the anvil and stolen goods. Fortunately, all of its inhabitants were gathered together — he wouldn't have any trouble returning their belongings. Unfortunately, they seemed ready to depart on an ogre-hunting expedition. They carried torches, pitchforks, swords, crossbows — any weapon they could find.

When they saw him coming, the villagers took a step back in fear. Then they looked at one another and at the weapons in their hands. They frowned at the ogre and raised them into the air.

"Now, hang on a minute," said Shrek. He stepped up and dropped the stolen items onto the ground. "Here's some of your stuff. If you want, I can lead you back to the hidden cave and show you the squirrel bandits who stole your things in the first place."

"Are you still talking about masked squirrels and magic caves?" asked a woman holding a rolling pin.

"Who would believe such a wild tale?" asked a man. He thumped a club into his open palm.

"You should," Shrek answered, "if you want your stuff back."

The villagers grumbled to one another.

"Now see here." Shrek placed his hands on his hips. "I'll take you to their hideout and you'll leave me alone. Do we have a deal?"

"Here's your answer, ogre," a voice said.

Shrek ducked as a wooden bolt zipped over his head. It stopped with a *TWANG* as it lodged into a nearby tree. The ogre looked up to see a man reloading his crossbow.

"Fine," said Shrek. "We'll do this the hard way."

The ogre spun around and dove for the bushes. Arrows and pitchforks flew after him.

Shrek barreled through the swamp and the villagers chased after him. One way or another, he planned to lead them to the rodent robbers and their hidden hideout. If they had to hunt him down to do it, so be it.

Shrek thought it was a brilliant plan. However, it had one major flaw — the villagers had absolutely no tracking skills whatsoever. Several times the ogre had to stop and wait for the angry mob to catch up to him. Sometimes they took off in the wrong direction completely. He had to keep doubling back, getting their attention, ducking as they shot at him, then continuing on toward the cave.

Shrek finally gave up when he circled back and found them shooting arrows into a large bush.

It's time for Plan B, he thought.

EIGHT

S hrek trudged back to the cave. If he couldn't lead the villagers to the bandits, he would take the bandits to the villagers. That was Plan B.

When he finally reached the secret hideout, he politely knocked on the boulder.

"Open Centipede!" said a voice from inside the cave.

The ogre stepped back as the boulder rolled aside. With swords already drawn, the captain and the two other squirrels leaped through the entryway.

"So, the thief returns to the scene of the crime!"

the captain announced as he pointed his sword at Shrek.

"Is that right?" Shrek asked. "Well, right now, the entire village is scouring the swamp looking for me. They think *I'm* the one stealing from them."

"And your point is?" asked the squirrel.

"My point is you three are the real thieves," Shrek argued. "And I'm going to prove it!"

The three squirrels made a circle around the ogre. "I don't think so," said the captain. His tail flicked anxiously. "I have other plans."

Shrek chuckled. "What are you going to do, make me spin the wheel?" he asked. "Well, let me warn you, you'll need an awful lot of badgers if you're going to give me the Whoa-Nelly."

"Badgers?" The captain bared his teeth. "We don't need any stinking badgers!"

Shrek knelt down and looked the captain in the eye. "Well, just what are three wee squirrels going to do against one great big ogre?"

The captain and the other squirrels glanced at one another, then burst into laughter. "Three of us?" asked the captain. "You'd better guess again."

Shrek heard a rustling in the bushes around him. He slowly stood upright and glanced around. Squirrels slowly crawled out of the undergrowth. They climbed down trees. They poured out of the open cave. Soon there were squirrels everywhere. Each of them glared and snarled at the ogre. And each carried a razor-sharp sword.

The captain laughed harder as the rest of his horde surrounded Shrek. "There aren't just three of us, ogre," he boasted. "There are *forty* of us!"

The squirrels drew their swords and aimed them at Shrek.

NINE

Shrek was surrounded. Even armed with swords, three tiny squirrels were no match for a giant ogre. Forty, on the other hand, was a different story. He may still win the battle, but those squirrels might do some heavy damage before it was through. They hissed and snarled as they encircled him and inched closer.

"Any last requests?" asked the captain of the bandits.

"Actually," said Shrek, "I do have one question."

"What is it?" barked the captain.

"Why would a bunch of squirrels steal all that junk in the first place?"

"Are you kidding?" asked the captain. His eye brightened. "This may be mere junk to you, but we make a fortune selling this stuff on treeBay!"

The rest of the squirrels chittered their agreement.

"You should see how much I got for this delightful four-piece dinner set," said one squirrel. "You could say I made out like . . . well, like a bandit!"

The forty squirrels burst into laughter.

Shrek took that opportunity to leap over the bandits and disappear into the trees.

"Get him!" the captain yelled behind him.

Shrek dashed through the swamp. He tromped through bogs, ducked under branches, and leaped over large bushes. Unfortunately, the forty armed squirrels were close behind him. They didn't keep their pursuit to the ground, either. Most of them bounded from tree to tree over the ogre's head.

Shrek jumped over one that pounced in front of him. He dodged another that fell from a tree. He even leaned backwards as a squirrel swung past on a vine. It swiped at the ogre with his sword, but missed.

That's not a bad idea, Shrek thought. He came to the edge of a large ravine and grabbed a vine of his own. He swung across as the squirrels skidded to a halt behind him. Happy to have gained some distance, Shrek looked back and smiled. His smile faded when he saw several of the tiny thieves climb smaller vines and begin to swing after him.

Still trying to outrun the swarm of squirrels, Shrek stumbled onto an old trail. He quickly followed it and poured on the speed. Up ahead, the trail shot to the left in front of a thick mass of thorny bushes. He quickly thought of an idea to shake the rampaging rodents. It wasn't going to be easy, but it just might work.

Instead of turning left with the trail, Shrek dove, headfirst, into the prickly shrubbery. Maybe the squirrels would keep following the trail.

"Ow-ow-ow-ow-ow!" Shrek cried as the large thorns scraped his skin.

When he burst out the other side, the ogre did a somersault and landed in a crouch. He waited quietly and listened for the pack of squirrels. They fell for it. Instead of following him, they continued down the trail.

"That's better," Shrek said with a sigh.

He was about to stand when he looked up and saw that he was completely surrounded by the angry villagers. They snarled and leveled their weapons at him.

"Plan C?" Shrek asked himself.

The ogre dove through another bush amid a barrage of arrows, axes, and angry shouts.

Once again, it was the villagers' turn to pursue the ogre through the swamp. Shrek ran, but he wasn't too concerned. He easily pulled away from the angry mob. At least they couldn't leap from tree to tree!

Suddenly, a squirrel burst from the underbrush and landed in front of him. The rodent swung his sword, but Shrek bounded over him and kept running.

"Over here!" the squirrel cried.

Soon the full force of the squirrels swarmed all around him. They nipped at his heels, they leaped from branch to branch overhead, and they scurried up the tree trunks on either side of him. They were like an army of ants, pouring over everything in their path.

With the pack of squirrels almost upon him and the mob of villagers behind them, Shrek had to take drastic action — fast!

He saw a tall tree up ahead and he got another idea. It was a risky move, but it was his only chance. Shrek ran faster and put a little distance between him and the swarming squirrels. It wasn't much, but it would have to be enough.

When he reached the tree, he jumped as hard as he could. He caught the lowest branch with both hands and hauled himself up. Shrek continued to scramble through the branches as he made his way up the tree. He felt the trunk rock as the squirrels hit like a whirlwind. He didn't have to look down to know that they were clambering up after him. After all, climbing trees was what squirrels did best. In fact, he was counting on it.

As Shrek neared the top, he could hear leaves rustling and small branches snapping below him. The forty thieves were closing in. When he finally reached the tip-top, he dared to look down. The squirrels covered every inch of the tiny branches below him. Many hissed as they drew their swords. They glared up at him and slowly climbed closer.

The captain crawled over the backs of the others to be the first to attack the ogre. Once he was in front, seventy-nine beady little eyes stared angrily at Shrek.

"You're a fool, ogre," announced the captain. "You can't escape this way. We squirrels are at home in the trees. Everyone knows that!" He drew his own sword.

"Let's see about that," Shrek replied. Holding tight to the treetop, he shifted all his weight to one side.

The tree jerked with him. The captain and several others dropped their swords as they grabbed the trunk and branches with all four paws.

Shrek wrenched his body in the other direction and the tree bent with him. When it slowed, he tugged it the other way. Soon the large tree swayed back and forth.

Shrek looked down. The villagers had gathered around the base of the tree. They pointed to the ogre and the pack of squirrels. Some even examined a few of the tiny swords that fell to the ground.

Shrek turned his attention to the captain of the bandits. The squirrel's claws scraped across the bark as the tree swayed back and forth. Shrek kept shifting his weight, making the tree tip lower and lower each time.

"Isn't this fun?" Shrek asked the captain.

The rest of the squirrels had fear in their eyes. But not the captain. He glared at Shrek with his one good eye and bared his two long teeth. With his claws dug into the tree, he still lifted one paw and pulled himself closer.

"You'll pay for this!" he growled.

Shrek kept tilting the tree until its tip nearly touched the ground on both sides. On the last pass, Shrek casually stepped off. He held onto the treetop, keeping it bent over.

"How about the old Up, Up, and Away?" Shrek asked the captain.

The captain's rage turned to fear. "Not Up, Up, and Away!" he pleaded. "Anything but that!"

Shrek smiled. "Up . . . up . . ." He let go of the treetop. "And *away!*"

The tree snapped back into place. It stopped — but the squirrels didn't. The tree shot the forty thieves into the air like a giant catapult. The band of bandits squealed as they sailed above the treetops. They kept going and going until they disappeared over the horizon.

"I didn't know they were *flying* squirrels," Shrek said with a chuckle.

TEN

 S hrek led the villagers back to the hidden cave. To their amazement, he said the secret password and the boulder magically rolled aside. After a little hesitation, a few stepped inside and retrieved their stolen belongings.

"We're very sorry, Mr. Ogre," said the man holding a pitchfork.

"We were wrong about you," said the blacksmith. "I guess forty squirrels can haul away an anvil if they wanted to."

"Fine, fine," said Shrek. "If you're all done here, I'll just be on my way."

A woman holding several plates ran up to him. "But how will we repay you?" she asked.

Shrek waved her away. "There's no need for that."

Another man walked out of the cave and toward the ogre. He carried a crossbow in one hand and two croquet mallets in the other. "We have to do *something* for you."

Shrek held up both hands. "No, really, that's quite all right."

A small group of villagers began to gather around the ogre. Shrek felt very uneasy about how comfortable they now seemed around him.

The woman with the dishes turned to the others. "I know!" she said. "We could have a parade!"

"Excellent idea!" someone agreed.

"Or maybe an honorary ball," suggested another.

"And a special award!"

"The key to the village!"

Shrek couldn't take any more. "All right!" he yelled. Everyone jumped with a start. "There *is* one thing you can do for me."

"What is it?" asked the blacksmith.

"All I want . . ." Shrek said quietly.

"Yes?" asked the woman.

". . . is to be left . . ." he continued.

"Yes?" asked the man with the mallets.

Shrek took a deep breath. "*ALOOOOOOOOOO-OOOOOOOOONE!*" he roared.

The villagers scattered in all directions. With armloads of recovered items, they dashed into the swamp and out of sight.

Shrek smiled. Things were back to normal. They were frightened of him again and he could live in peace.

As he began to return home himself, something caught his eye. Shrek bent over and spotted a very small patch of green-ring toadstools. He plucked them from the ground and placed them safely in his pocket. There weren't many of them, but it looked as if he would have his special treat after all.

"The end," said Shrek. "That's it. End of story."

Donkey jumped to his feet. "Oh, my! What a *believable* story, Shrek," he said sarcastically. "It had everything! Suspense . . . intrigue . . . and I'm sure it was *all* true."

Shrek grumbled as he got to his feet. He grabbed a battered frying pan from a hook near the fireplace. "This is the very pan they stole from me."

Donkey rolled his eyes. "Oh, well, that proves it." He turned his back to the ogre. "The next time I want to hear a tall tale," he mumbled, "I'll go hang with Pinocchio!"

Shrek dropped the pan and put his hands on his hips. "Oh, so I'm lying now, am I?"

Donkey spun around. "I don't need to see your nose growing to tell me that!"

Fiona jumped in between them. "Boys, boys, please!" She placed both hands on Shrek's shoulders. "I think it was a wonderful story. Very exciting."

Shrek gazed into her eyes. "You believe me, don't you?"

"Of course I do, dear," she replied.

"Well, that makes one of us," Donkey announced.

Shrek was about to reply when Fiona placed a hand on his lips. "Why don't you go get some more fire-wood?" He tried to speak but Fiona interrupted him. "A long walk may do you good."

Shrek sighed. "You're right." He gave her a hug, then stepped through the front door.

"I think I'll go, too," said Donkey.

"Be nice," Fiona warned.

The little donkey swished his tail. "I will, I will." He trotted out the door. "Maybe we'll run into this *magic cave*."

Donkey quickly caught up to Shrek. The two didn't speak as they traveled deeper into the swamp.

Finally, Donkey broke the silence. "Okay, I just have one question," he said.

Shrek shook his head. "What's that?"

"If your story is true, and the bandits aren't there anymore, why didn't you use the cave?" he asked. "Maybe for storage, or a nice summer home or something."

"I don't know, really," Shrek replied. He reached down and picked up a broken tree branch. "Probably because I forgot the password ages ago."

Donkey stopped in his tracks. "Wait a minute. I thought you said the password was *Open Centipede!*"

Shrek halted as well. "Now I *did* make up that part of the story," he admitted. "I didn't remember the real password and I couldn't just say *Open Something-something*, now could I?"

"Was the real password the name of a bug, too?" asked Donkey.

Shrek thought for a moment. "No, I think it was some kind of grain."

Donkey's ears perked up. "Grain? I'm a donkey. I know all about grain!" Shrek continued into the swamp and Donkey followed. He cocked his head to one side. "Was it *Open Barley?*"

"No," Shrek replied. "That wasn't it."

Donkey thought some more. "How about *Open Wheat?*"

"Nope."

"*Alfalfa?*"

"Not it, either."

"How about *Sesame?*" asked Donkey. "That kind of sounds like *Centipede.*"

"*Open Sesame?*" Shrek said with a chuckle. "Now that's just silly."

Donkey and Shrek strolled through the swamp. Neither of them noticed when, behind them, a vine-covered boulder slowly and magically rolled away from the mouth of a hidden cave.